The Pickpocket and the Princess

A. Carys

A. Carys

The characters and events portrayed in this book are fictitious. Any similarity to real persons, living or dead, is coincidental and not intended by the author.

No part of this book may be reproduced, or stored in a retrieval system, or transmitted in any form or by any means, electronic, mechanical, photocopying, recording, or otherwise, without express written permission of the publisher.

Copyright © 2024 A. Carys

All rights reserved.

BOOKS IN THIS SERIES

Of Doors and Betrayal

The Pickpocket and the Princess

The Master, My Wings, Our Service

'Cos This Is How Villains Are Made

A Circus of Wonder

A Sentence to Death

A Deal With The Devil

Let Her Go

The Three

Queen Rory, The Banished

A. Carys

The Pickpocket and the Princess

DEDICATION

Today is a good day, and tomorrow it's going to rain.

A. Carys

CHAPTER ONE

Pickpockets.

They're quick. Sneaky. And most of the time, you don't realise they've taken anything until you get home.

I'm not a pickpocket. My job isn't even remotely close to that of a pickpocket's, but I do know some tricks of the trade. I was taught by a girl called Chrissy and we would practice around the docks where she lives. She liked to cause mischief, especially when we were growing up, so she taught me how to pick pockets without getting caught. But it's been years since Chrissy and I were children, we're all grown up now, and the time for childish mischief is over.

But on the night of the Molleni Star Festival, a

night where I should be preparing to wish upon the Wishing Star, the emptiness inside of my chest gets the better of me and I decide to try my luck. And somehow, instead of trying to steal from a normal islander, I try to steal from a princess.

"How dare you," she whisper-yells as she pushes my face into the gravel. It cuts into the skin on my cheek, making me wince.

"It's nothing personal," I tell her.

"Oh, I think it is. Do you know who I am?"

"Can't really tell since you've got my face against the gravel. It'd be greatly appreciated if you could let me go."

She scoffs. "Let you go? You need to be arrested."

"Is that so?"

"Yes. I'm waiting for a policeman to wander by. This event is heavily protected you kno–"

She squeals as I kick her in the ankle. She falls backwards and I use her distracted state to quickly manoeuvre myself onto my feet. She looks me dead in the eyes and I know exactly what she's about to do; so I don't let her. Grabbing her by the arm, I push her against the wall. One hand covering her mouth, while the other grabs her wrists, pinning them above her head.

"You know, I do recognize you. Your Royal Highness, Princess Katarina."

She glares at me, and I feel her mouth move underneath my hand. I raise an eyebrow at her, challenging her. She seems to accept the challenge as I feel her graze her teeth across the palm of my hand. I shake my head and firmly flatten my hand so she can't move her mouth at all.

"That's not very nice, now is it? Biting me."

She mumbles something against my hand, her eyebrows furrowed and her eyes furiously boring into mine. I smile and since I'm curious to know what she said, I remove my hand.

"Holding the Crown Princess against her will is treason, I'll have you hanged for this," she repeats, but I'm not convinced that's how she really feels. Her angry expression tells me one thing, but a little glint of mischief in her eyes tells me another.

"Will you now?" I challenge.

She hesitates. "Yes."

"Sure?"

"Yes. Maybe."

"Make up your mind princess, because depending on your answer, you might not make it home tonight."

Her eyes widen. "Where would you put me if I said yes?" she asks, sucking in a deep breath.

"My home. The guest bedroom, to be specific. I'd put iron bars over the windows and hold you for ransom. I'd lock the door in such a way that you wouldn't be able to get out unless I let you."

"Really?" she asks, breathless. She's either panicking, or enjoying this just as much as I am, which makes me think that Princess Katarina isn't as innocent as her parents paint her to be.

"Yes. But I'm also a gracious host, so I'd keep you company during mealtime."

"What would we eat?"

I smile at her. "Whatever you wanted. I'm quite the chef."

"Oh yeah?"

"Yeah," I say, bringing my face a little closer to hers. Our noses only a centimetre from touching.

"What if I didn't know what I wanted to eat?"

"Then I'd start with my mother's favourite meal. Brown rice with mixed peas, sweetcorn and pepper chunks. All nicely simmering in a reduced sauce of subtle mixed spices."

"Sounds heavenly."

"It is. My mother was the best chef. She taught me all she knew."

She takes a deep breath and I make the distance between our faces a little bigger. "Are you really going to do that? Keep me locked in your house?" Her voice is softer now, calmer.

"No, but only if you agree to let me see you again."

"You want to see me again? Even after I shoved your face into the gravel and threatened to have you killed?"

I smile at her. "Call it a story for the grandkids."

She laughs. Her laugh is enchanting, captivating. "You're deluded."

"I know," I step back, letting her go completely. "But you love it."

"I don't even know you."

"You could get to know me, if you agree to meet

me again."

She smiles at me. "Where should we meet?"

I smile and shove my hands in my pockets. "The Rat and Mouse."

"The Rat and Mouse?"

"Every pickpocket, lowly criminal and my team's favourite den. It's hidden, but if you ask the right person on Sal Street, they'll let you in."

"Do I need a name?"

I raise an eyebrow at her.

"Will I need to tell someone I know you to be let in?" she says, looking me in the eyes as she waits for my answer.

"Fallon. I don't get a lot of visitors, but I'll let them know I'm expecting a princess," I say as I step back, letting her go. She smooths her long skirt and pulls down the corset she's wearing.

She smiles, nodding, before walking away. I wait to see if she will look back, and she does, giving me a small wave. I wink at her before heading in the opposite direction.

I slink about in the shadows, bypassing the Police Officers who are working on crowd control. I slip through a small alleyway and into the shadow covered Sal Street.

"Fallon, what are you doin' here so late?" asks Old Monty. He's sitting in his favourite corner, his rocking chair creaking as it moves.

Old Monty, a man who has sat in the same chair, on the same street corner for the last five years. He's the keeper of Sal Street, the main high street where the Rat and Mouse is located. He doesn't let in anyone he hasn't seen before, and he sure as hell doesn't let Police Patrols push their way through to arrest anyone.

"I'll be waiting for a date. With a princess," I say with a wink.

Monty laughs. "Only you Fallon, only you."

"What can I say? I'm a hit."

Monty shakes his head, laughing. I wave him goodbye as I step into the warm pub.

For three nights, I sit in my favourite booth in the Rat and Mouse, patiently waiting for Katarina. The very centre booth with its carved table and purple backed benches.

My head snaps in the direction of the door as it swings open. My eyes land on Katarina and a smile tugs at my lips. Part of me didn't think she'd come, that she'd stand me up because she didn't fancy involving herself with a sort of criminal. But here she is, standing there looking like a fish out of water.

She timidly looks around the pub, her eyes scanning over every table and booth until she spots me. As she marches over to the booth, I take a quick glance at her attire. She's wearing a similar outfit to the one she wore the night we met. This time though, she has a black cape draped over her body and hood caging her face.

"Hi," she says, taking a seat at my booth.

"Hey," I respond as I watch her settle.

In the pub light, I get a better look at her, far better than in that darkened alleyway. She removes her hood to reveal the most beautiful head of black curls. They frame her face and as the light catches them, they shimmer, appearing an almost midnight blue. The mixture of colours really bring out her eyes, and they also bring out the natural red tint to her lips. Her skin is unblemished and looks so soft. She's gorgeous, and my heart speeds up at every thought that rushes through my mind.

"Are you okay?" she asks, bringing me out of my daydreaming.

I nod. "Glad to see you took me up on my offer. Did curiosity get the better of you?"

She smiles. "More like morbid curiosity."

"Why morbid?"

"Because if my parents find out about this, you'll be killed," she whispers, looking down at her hands.

"We'll just have to be careful," I say, reassuring her as I take hold of one of her hands. "Your hands are soft."

"Years of being kept in a palace, and a good overnight moisturizer," she says, half-joking.

We're silent for a moment.

"Can I ask you something, princess?"

"Kat, please call me Kat. And yes, anything."

"Why were you out the other night?"

"I wanted to see the festival up close. My parents never took me to see the festival in person, we had to watch from the palace balcony or not at all. They were on the Mainland at the time, so I took a chance." She takes a breath. "What about you, why were you there?"

"This isn't about me," I say.

"I told you why I was out, it's only fair you tell me why you were out."

"Fair enough. I was going to pray upon the Wishing Star, that night marked five years since the passing of my father. Unfortunately I couldn't bring myself to pray, so I decided to try and steal from a princess."

"I'm sorry to hear about your father." I nod and squeeze her hand.

"What about tonight? What made you come meet me?" I ask, changing the subject.

I watch her throat work before she answers.

"You."

I'm surprised, but also not. "Me?"

"The other night, I felt alive. We fought, we argued, and then we talked. I felt things that I'd never felt before, and I wanted to know more. Wanted to know why."

"What did you feel?" I question, leaning back against the booth and letting go of her hand.

"Please don't make me say it, it's embarrassing," she hisses as the waitress places down our drinks. I nod in thanks and take a sip of my usual, spiced wine with an undertone of sweet berries. For Kat, I ordered a water, not knowing if she was one to drink.

"I'd like to know what brought you here, unless you're a chicken," I say, challenging her.

She glares at me, which makes me smirk. I've known her for a matter of hours but learning what makes her tick is suddenly everything to me. I want to know all of the things she felt the other night, and I want to know what she's feeling right now. I want to know what she's scared of and what she loves. I want to know everything about her.

"But I think I can fill in the gaps."

She lets out, what I assume to be, a sigh of relief.

"You can?"

"Yes. You felt alive–"

"I already told you–"

"Don't interrupt," I order, and she instantly shuts her mouth. "You felt alive, ignited even. Like you'd awoken something inside of yourself. You liked fighting with me, you liked challenging me and you liked it when I had you up against—"

She slaps her hands over my mouth as she slides around the booth.

"Please, it's embarrassing."

I shake my head and pull her hands away, tucking them under the table.

"It's not embarrassing. You've grown up knowing what was expected of you and you weren't given the chance to experience anything else. You haven't had the chance to fall in love properly or explore relationships, and you've not been given the chance to explore who you are. To find the real you. But the other night woke a side of you that you might never have discovered if you'd just been chucked at a prince."

She purses her lips. "I have been chucked at a prince. Prince Miles."

"I take it from your tone that you don't want to marry Prince Miles?"

"I don't want to marry him. He's awful to be around and he's picked on me since we were children.

I've told my father I don't want to marry Miles, but he says he doesn't care. Says that it's my duty to marry a prince before I become Queen."

I nod. "What do you want?"

"Is it too early to say you?"

"No."

"Then you. I want you."

Butterflies explode inside me.

We finish our drinks, chatting and getting to know each other, before leaving the pub. I pull her through the back roads until she stops me.

"What's wrong?"

"Nothing, nothing. I just– ugh, god why is this so ugh– why don't you come back to the palace with me?" she asks shyly, looking down at her feet.

I bite my lip as I reach out and lift her chin. "Kat, are you asking me to spend the night with you?"

She whines. "Please don't make me say it again."

"If you don't ask, I don't know what you want."

She rolls her eyes. "Will you spend the night with me?" she murmurs. She tries to move her chin off my finger, attempting to shy away. But I don't let her as I press my thumb against her chin, trapping her face.

"I'm sorry, I didn't quite catch that."

She takes a deep breath. "Fallon, would you like to spend the night with me?"

"I would like nothing more."

She smiles brightly before grabbing my hand and pulling me along behind her. She sneaks me into the palace. We run through hidden passageways, following them from the lower walls of the palace all the way up to Kat's bedroom.

We spend the night together. The both of us snuggled up under her duvet, content in our own world. In the morning, just before her maids come and help her dress for the day, she sneaks me out the same way we came in.

"When can I see you again?" she asks as I step away from her.

"Whenever you want, just say."

"Come back tonight? I can meet you by the willow tree at the bottom of the hill."

"Perfect," I say as I lean forward and brush a kiss against her lips. "See you tonight."

CHAPTER TWO

I wake up tangled in Kat's sheets.

She's next me, curled into my side with the duvet tucked up right under her chin. She's adorable when she sleeps, and I've been lucky to wake up next to her every day for the last month.

We've done a lot together since establishing our relationship nine months ago. Two months of dates and getting to know each other turned into nine months of a secret relationship. Frankly, being with Kat for the last eleven months have been the best months of my life, especially since the anniversary of my father's death left me feeling empty. Being with Kat seems to have filled most of the emptiness that sat deep within me, and I couldn't be more grateful for her.

Together, we've explored the Island. We've told each other our deepest thoughts and secrets. She's become my best friend and the love of my life. Our souls feel so deeply wound together that I'm convinced meeting in the alley was always meant to happen. I'm convinced that Kat is my soulmate, and I don't use that term lightly.

We've also become so deeply entrenched in each other's lives that I can't remember a time when I didn't know Kat. Not like I do now at least. And in the time we've been together I've watched Kat grow into the perfect future Queen. She's taken quite an interest in the issues facing the citizens of Molleni. She's partaken in some reconstruction work my team has been doing on buildings around the island, and she's sat and listened to their concerns. She's already showing the citizens how she intends to rule, and every time I think about it, deep pride settles in my chest.

Kat will be good for Molleni and its Associated Territories. She knows what the people want, what they need. She can also work on reversing her father's ridiculous laws, all of which have been influenced by a sudden change in the way he rules over us. The sudden paranoia about certain Island visitors, and his unexpected need for everyone to be in their houses by a certain time. And you can't ignore all the twitching and ticks he appears to have during public appearances. Something isn't right with the King, and while I've been ignoring those things while I've been spending time with Kat, I've not forgotten them.

Kat and I have said we love each other, and we've been domestic together. We've worked around each other like a married couple; even if we can't leave the confines of her bedroom for fear of being discovered. I've given my heart to her completely, and she's given me hers. But things are complicated now. Prince Miles has been staying in the visitor wing of the palace. He's ready to stake his claim as the next King Consort of Molleni Island and Associated Territories. But that isn't what Kat wants, and I wish I could provide the solution.

"We could run away," she mutters, stretching with a yawn.

"If we did, we'd never be able to come back," I

say and place a kiss on the crown of her head.

She sighs. "I don't want to disappoint my family, but I also don't want to lose you."

"You won't lose me. What did I tell you after our first night together?"

"That I was it for you."

"And I meant it. We'll get through this, and I'll wait for you if I have to. Once you're Queen, you can do anything you want."

"But what–"

"Katarina? Are you awake?" Marnie, her Lady in Waiting and *second* best friend, asks through the locked door.

We look at each other with panic. The both of us sit up against the headboard and scramble to pull the duvet over our bodies. While we've told Marnie we've been seeing each other, we haven't told her the extent of our relationship. And I'm pretty sure her walking in and finding us both naked isn't on her to-do list today.

Although, that wouldn't be the end of the world considering I've known Marnie for quite some time. A time previous to my relationship with Kat. She's part of the group I'm in charge of. A group devoted to righting the wrongs the King and Queen have partaken in against the island. As head, and daughter of the founder, I'm there to oversee the smoothness of every job. I have eight groups who all have a different set of skills, and when it comes to handing out jobs, I leave it to the leaders of those groups. We work with the people and for the people. I'm just the one controlling the money, the permits, the developmental projects and the controlled protests. It's what my father would've wanted, a new sense of freedom brought to the people of Molleni Island. And as of late, Kat has become a vital member of the group.

"I swear, Katarina, one day I'm going to remove the lock from this door– woah, oh god," she gasps as she comes into the room, her eyes briefly glancing over us. She covers her eyes.

"Really? Today of all days?"

"Yes?" Kat says, smiling.

"Marnie, lock the door." She locks the door.

"How long?"

"What?" Kat asks.

"How long have you been doing this for?"

"Two nights after we met. You knew that anyway," I say to her.

"I knew you two were seeing each other, not *sleeping* together. Dear god. Seriously?"

I grin, feeling very happy with myself as I wrap an arm around Kat's shoulders. "Seriously."

"Well, as cute as that is, I need you two to get dressed. The King and Queen expect Kat in the dining room in twenty minutes."

Kat groans beside me before burying her face in my shoulder. I kiss the crown of her head before running my hand through the hair at the base of her neck. I carefully grasp the tight curls and gently pull her head from my shoulder.

"It'll be okay. I'll come back tonight, and you can tell me all about it."

"Okay," she murmurs before leaning up and pressing a chaste kiss to my lips.

"Uh uh, nope. You can't come back tonight," Marnie says, panic lacing her voice. I get up from the bed and grab my shirt and underwear.

"What do you mean I can't come back tonight?"

"The King and Queen are having Kat move into

Prince Miles' room tonight. The engagement announcement is happening this afternoon."

I stop getting dressed and go stand directly in front of Marnie.

"What's going on? Tell me the short version," I say in a lower tone so only Marnie can hear me.

"The royals are worried, specifically the king. They know about the next round of protests, today's to be specific, and with the upcoming Official Gathering being held on the Island, they don't want questions being asked by the Territories," she says, lowly.

"But why rush the engagement?"

"To show stability. A new generation of Kings and Queens would prove that the island is fine. That there isn't any instability within the royal family," she says.

I run a hand through my hair as I nod. "Tell today's group to lay low, get off the streets, but have the construction teams keep going. They have their permits so there shouldn't be any issues."

"Will do."

"Thank you, Marnie."

"Don't thank me until you're out of here.

Camille's team will be here soon." With that, she unlocks the door and leaves. I relock it behind her, not wanting anyone else walking in.

"Fal?"

I walk over to the bed. "I'm here. What do you need?"

"I want to tell them."

"Your parents?"

"Yes. I want to tell them about us."

"Are you sure?"

"Yes. I don't want to marry Miles, he's slimy and quite sexist, no matter how charming he may seem. And I don't want to be apart from you."

"I don't want that either, but we'll only do it if you're one hundred percent sure."

"I'm more than one hundred percent sure, this is what I want. I want you, a life with *you*."

I quickly collect the rest of my discarded clothes before hiding in the bathroom while Camille's team gets Kat ready. She's told me herself she hates when they arrive every morning to pull and prod at her. She'd prefer to do it herself. One morning, she asked me to plait her hair, and that went down as well as expected once her parents saw it.

"You can come out now," Kat says, opening the bathroom door.

"Are you sure you want to do this?" I ask as I pull her to me.

"Yes. I don't want to hide us anymore."

"Then lead the way."

We hold hands all the way to the dining room. When we enter, the King and Queen are seated at either end, with Prince Miles in the middle. My stomach rumbles at the sight of all of the food that lines the fabric runner.

"Katarina, who is this?" asks King Kieran. We stare at each other, sizing the other up. I watch as Kieran's eyes flicker with emotion and his head twitches.

"This is Fallon."

"And what is *Fallon* doing at family breakfast?" Queen Camille asks, the distaste in her tone obvious.

"I wanted you to meet her because I don't want to marry Miles. Fallon and I have been together for the last year, and I want to be with her. I *belong* with her," Kat announces as she squeezes the life out of my hand.

"Katarina don't be silly. You've not been in a relationship with Fallon. Miles is the one you belong to," Camille says, dismissing her daughter completely.

"No, mother. I love Fallon. I'm not going to be marrying Miles because eventually I'll marry Fallon."

Her parents look at each other before they burst out laughing. "Kat, sweetheart, you don't get that choice. The Crown Princess will marry a suitor, preferably a prince, of her parents choosing in order to keep the Royal line as pristine as possible," Kieran says, his hands twitching over his plate.

"That's archaic," I say, finally bored of their attitude toward Kat.

"No one was talking to you, Miss–"

"Edington." The Queen smiles smarmily at me.

"Edington. It's been what, five years since we've seen your father? How is he doing?"

I take a deep breath, resisting the urge to roll my eyes. "He's still dead, thanks for asking."

"Guards," the King calls and the room fills with the Royals personal guard. "Take Miss Edington and hold her in the cells. I will deal with her shortly," he orders.

"No, do not touch her," Kat squeals. She moves her arms and tries to keep the guards away from me.

"Katarina. Let the guards deal with her."

"NO. She's mine," she yells and that makes me smile. *Hers*.

The guards grab Kat by her wrists and chuck her to the side.

"Don't chuck her, she is your princess," I snarl as they take hold of me, feeling extremely possessive and protective over Kat.

I attempt to batter a guard with my fist but fail. The guards are far stronger than I am. They guide me away, letting the tips of my shoes drag across the floor.

"NO," Kat yells again before appearing in front of me. "Fal, please don't go." Tears brim at her eyes as I smile at her.

"I'll be fine. I'm always fine."

"But–"

"But nothing. You'll get through this, and I'll be waiting for you on the other side. Okay?"

She nods. "Okay." She doesn't walk away right away, instead she comes toe to toe with me before grabbing my face in her hands and pulling me down to kiss her.

It feels like a final kiss. Like she thinks we'll never see each other again. But we will, I'm determined to see her again. Nothing will ever keep us apart.

"Be safe."

"You too."

The guards guide me away, taking me down staircase after staircase until we reach a row of cells. They push me into the closest cell and lock it.

"The King will be with you shortly."

"Lucky me."

※

I don't know how long I sit in this cell, but the longer I wait, the more pissed off I feel myself becoming.

The guards keep coming back to check on me, as though they think I'm going to escape. And believe me, I looked, but this place has one way in and one way out.

"Fallon Edington. Daughter of disgraced Politician Luke Edington. A man who managed to steal four million Orden over the course of a forty year career."

I roll my eyes. "Paul Eatons did that, not my father. I have the evidence to prove it," I say to him. While my father may not have stolen that money, he did manage to get his hands on it days before he passed. He then left it to me, in an account under my name. The account came with a single note that told me to *'finish what he started'*.

Kieran chuckles and his head twitches to the left. "I bet you do, but you won't be needing it."

I roll my eyes, knowing that he doesn't mean he believes that my father didn't do it. "And why's that?"

He motions to the guards who come forward. They open the door to the cell and usher me out so that I'm standing in front of Kieran. I stand with a straight back, my shoulders back and my eyes boring into his in an attempt to show that I'm not scared of him. That he cannot bully me into submission by bringing up my father or trapping me in a cell.

"Because you won't be around to need it," he says as he brandishes a blade, immediately stabbing me in the stomach. "And Miles will take great care of Katarina, that I can assure you."

He lets me fall down onto my back, the blade scratching away at my insides. I pant and groan as I try to save myself, but it's no use. Kieran smirks at me as he watches me writhe in pain. He tells the guards to leave me to bleed out and only after I take my final breath may they move my body and bury it in a shallow grave.

I watch him turn his back, his hands twitching, and fingers locking up. He slowly walks towards the stone staircase and leaves, taking his guards with him.

I try to put pressure on the wound one last time, even though I realise that I'm unlikely to make it out of here alive.

"FALLON."

I let my head loll to the side and see Marnie barrelling down the steps. She's followed by Lita and Carlos. Lita and Carlos are also part of my network. They deal in information and keep me and my team leaders in the political loop. My network and group wouldn't have survived this long if it wasn't for them.

"Oh my god. Lita put pressure around the wound. Carlos give me your belt," Marnie orders.

"The next two minutes are going to hurt like hell, but we need to control the bleeding before we move you," Lita says as she presses down on either side of the wound.

"Argh, shit."

"Yep, just squeeze my hand." Carlos takes my hand as Marnie works on winding the belt around my stomach. She threads it and then pulls it tight, making me cry out. Pain ripples across my stomach and my vision blurs.

"She's going."

"NO. Fallon, stay with us."

My eyes won't stay open, and my body feels heavy and light at the same time.

"Fallon, please."

I let my eyes shut, and the darkness that has been playing at the edge of my vision takes over.

CHAPTER THREE

I lose count of how many days I spend staring at the ceiling.

I don't even know how many days I was unconscious for. What I do know is that my body aches. I have a pounding headache, and my heart feels like it's in a thousand tiny pieces.

"You're healing nicely, but I'd recommend another few weeks of limited movement," Lita tells me as she examines my stomach. I try to pull my head forwards and I manage to catch a brief glimpse of my stomach. The wound has scabbed across the middle, and a significant amount of stitches neatly hold the skin together. It looks rough, the skin around the wound red and mean looking.

"H-how long?" I croak, my throat dry as hell.

"Three weeks. It was touch and go for a while. Thought we were going to lose you."

"Infections?"

"None, thankfully. Benji's team really is the best on the Island."

"Internal damage?"

"A little bit. But Benji's assured me that he patched you up extremely well, all things considered."

I nod. "Where are we?"

"My cottage. Just outside the palace grounds."

"Kat? Where is she? What happened to her?"

"Still in the palace. The Royal Family have practically barricaded themselves inside. I've not been able to get near her."

"Why not?"

Lita sighs, looking away from me. She works on replacing the bandage around my torso before pulling my shirt back down.

"Lita, why not?" I ask again, becoming concerned about Kat's welfare.

"She's been ordered to stay in her wing of the palace. Miles was moved in two weeks ago, and since then, only certain members of staff have been allowed in. I've tried getting one of Marnie's team in the line-up of tending staff, but the changes keep being rejected."

"Has Marnie seen her?"

She shakes her head. "Marnie is being kept an eye on. The Royals don't trust her because they feel like she knew about you and Kat. In their eyes, Marnie should have told them what was going on the second she found out."

"She knew. Marnie was always going to find out because of how close she and Kat are. She helped us hide our relationship, she was never going to tell Kieran and Camille about us."

"I know she wouldn't. But right now things are tense, and Marnie hasn't been as active on the communication channels as usual."

"Is she still at the palace? And where's Carlos?"

"They're both at the palace. Marnie is laying low while Carlos is working on a way to get into the team looking after Kat. He's not sharing details in case people are listening."

I groan as I try to sit up.

"No, no. You need to lay down." She panics as

she tries to get me to lay back down. "You'll rip your stitches."

"I need to go to her. I need to make sure she's okay."

"I'll get Carlos to bring as much information as possible, but since they pushed back the engagement announcement there's no guarantee tha–"

Carlos bursts into the cottage. "They've just announced the engagement."

"No," I groan, and I push myself all the way up until I can lean against the headboard.

"They just radio broadcasted the news."

"Did they say anything else?" Lita asks as she goes back to checking my wound in case the sudden movements disturbed it.

"They'll be announcing the wedding date in a week's time."

"Lita, you have to get in to see Kat. I need to know she's okay," I say breathlessly as pain begins to curl in my stomach, right around the wound.

"I'll try tonight."

"Thank you."

"Now please lay down, you're going to pop a

stitch. Benji's out of town and you do not want me having a go at stitching you back up."

I nod and carefully slide back down so that I'm lying on my back. Lita walks off, probably to get some fresh air after the amount of panic attacks I've induced with my need to move.

"Carlos?" I call out as I stare at the ceiling again.

"Yes?"

"Tell me about Miles."

I feel him get on the bed, his sort of muscular frame taking up most of the right side of the bed. He doesn't say anything as he shuffles around, trying to get comfortable.

"Miles is, well, what you'd expect of the Prince of Ordol. Slimy. Righteous. Entitled."

"Have you seen him with her?"

"No. Looks like she isn't going down without a fight though. I heard from one her personal team that she punched him square in the jaw after he tried to make her walk behind him."

"That's my girl," I mutter, smiling with pride.

"She doesn't know what happened to you. No one knows, actually. Her parents have kept it under wraps."

I roll my eyes. "Course they did. In their eyes, I'm supposed to be nothing to Kat, merely a distraction because she *belongs to Miles*. It wouldn't change their opinion, but if they could've just see how our relationship was then maybe we could still be together. Even if it wasn't in an official, public way."

"You love her?"

"With everything I have. That girl has my heart and I have hers and I'm not letting her marry that prince."

"How are you going to stop the wedding? There'll be guards and levels of security that civilians with tickets will struggle to get through."

"I have at least one person in every single role in that palace. I have people that work in high places in parliament and as low level bottom feeders. I know everything because I have eyes and ears all over this bloody island. If anyone can get into that wedding, it's me."

I see him nod out of the corner of my eye. "What's the plan, boss?"

"Not sure, but when I have one, you'll be the first

to   know."

CHAPTER FOUR

Exactly seven days after Carlos told me the palace had announced the engagement, they announced the wedding date. Two weeks from now, Tuesday 5th March.

My stomach is still healing, but Benji is happy with the progress. The redness has gone down significantly, and I also got my stitches out yesterday, but I am under strict instructions from Benji to move with care.

In other news, both Carlos and Lita have been unsuccessful in getting to Kat, which means none of us have any idea how she is. It doesn't help that she was absent on the palace balcony during the wedding date broadcast. We're all on edge, and extremely concerned about her welfare. I'm worried that if I don't get someone to her soon, something bad is going to happen. That thought alone makes me feel sick.

"Are you sure Marnie is going to turn up?" Lita asks as we walk through the streets of Molleni. It looks a lot different in the late summer evenings, especially today because of the new curfews that were brought in. Since the palace is preparing for the wedding, and in order to secure all of the routes that the Royal carriages will be taking during the procession, they need everyone off the streets and in their homes by half eight. A whole hour earlier than the original curfews.

"I hope so," I respond as we head down the alley which will take us toward the Rat and Mouse. Marnie managed to get a cryptic note to the cottage, telling us to meet her there at nine - oh - clock.

"Glad to see ya up and 'bout, Fallon," Monty says as we pass by.

"Were you worried about me, Monty?" I tease.

"Of course. Never won't be worried 'bout you Fallon."

I smile at him.

"Don't make me cry Monty."

He laughs and shakes his head. "How's your girl?"

"Trapped, for now."

He raises his metal mug. "Well, here's to getting her back, and finally putting a ring on it."

I laugh, shaking my head at the same time at his antics.

The people in the community accepted Kat with open arms. They welcomed her, they made her feel safe. She got involved on the building sites when we went to visit. She took part in games with the children when we visited the newly converted schools. She showed them what they meant to her, and they showed her what she meant to them. Everyone's been waiting to hear news about how she's doing, and that is what keeps me going. There are people waiting for her, a whole other family who are waiting to welcome her back into their arms.

"I mean it. And when you do, I want a good seat at the wedding."

"Deal."

We head down the alley, right into the shadows that bathe the dead end. On the left sits the Rat and

Mouse, and with a flash of my pinkie ring, the bouncer on the door lets us in. It's not only the palace that has increased its security. Everyone who frequents the Rat and Mouse has been given a pinkie ring. The ring has become an ID of sorts, it helps the bouncers know who is allowed in, and who is to be questioned before entry.

We walk through the pub and take a seat in the centre booth.

"Time?" Lita asks. I check my pocket watch.

"8:45."

"It's a miracle we got here before curfew rounds began," Lita says as she gestures to a waitress.

"Patrols are low down here; there's too much land and the palace doesn't have the budget to secure every single street. Even if they temporarily hired people from the town, they don't know where people's loyalties lie."

"What can I get you ladies to drink tonight?"

"Three cinnamon spices please," I say without even looking up.

"Coming right up." The waitress walks off before returning minutes later with the drinks. In that time, we don't say anything. Despite this particular waitress, Carli, being on the payroll of the people who work for the people who work for me, they are still liable to eavesdropping and discussing what they heard with their friends later. And sometimes that is a risk we cannot take, especially with the topics that will be discussed in this meeting.

The minutes tick by and there's still no sign of Marnie.

"I'm worried, Fal. She's never late, not like this."

I look at my pocket watch. *9:25.*

"We don't know anything yet. Just be patient, Lita."

Lita was right.

Something is wrong. It's ten - oh - clock and Marnie still hasn't arrived.

"Carli?" I call out as I reach the bar.

"Hi, how can I help you?"

"Have there been any notes left for Fallon Edington or Lita Kiy?"

She looks behind the bar, in the hall where the desks are, and in the back office.

"No, sorry. Is everythin–"

"HELP. We need help."

I turn and see Monty with his arm wrapped around a bruised and bloodied person. I rush over, so do Carli and Lita. Monty lies the person down on the floor. They're limp and the only sign that they are still alive is the slight whimper that escapes them.

"Carli, grab me scissors, a bunch of washcloths and a bowl of lukewarm water." She runs off, and I work on talking to the person in front of me.

"Where does it hurt?"

"Everywhere."

Lita and I lock eyes.

"Marnie? Marnie, talk to me. What happened?"

"The palace. K-King Kieran. You need to do something," she murmurs, and she tries to look down at her body.

"Lita, talk to her, but keep her still."

Carli comes back with everything I told her to grab. I snatch the scissors from her before telling her to carefully take Marnie's shoes off. While she does that, I start cutting through the fabric of her top. I cut up the middle before cutting down both the arms. As I peel away her top, parts of the fabric stick to the wounds that are all over the front of her torso. I take away what I can without hurting her further, but they're very messy. They were clearly done quickly, and without care. They're jagged and vary in depth and length with fabric from her top sticking to them.

I place one palm on the back of my other hand before pressing down on her stomach. Marnie groans a little, but not enough to indicate that she has an internal injury. But to be on the safe side, I look to Monty.

"What ya need me to do?"

"Find Benji. He should be two buildings over. Command Street, house number 8. Tell him to bring blood and surgical equipment."

"Right ya're," he says as he leaves.

"Carli, I need you to put the closed sign up right now. We don't need any patrons coming in for late night drinks. Then, I need you to find me a first aid kit and something I can squirt water out of. I need to irrigate her wounds."

"Okay."

"What do you need me to do?" Lita asks.

"Tell me who did this."

"The King. She said that he found her talking to Kat, trying to warn her about what was going on."

"Warn her about what?"

"That the King is mobilising forces to shut down every work site you have people on, to shut down buildings that we've restored before they come for you. He knows you're alive and wants to stamp out the rising rebellion before we have a chance to act."

"He couldn't have Kat find out that I'm still alive, so he drags Marnie away and punishes her. Great," I summarise, nausea bubbling in my throat.

"This means that Kat is in danger." Panic sizzles under my skin at the prospect of Kat being in danger from her own father. But I force myself to push those feelings down since there's nothing I can do about that right this second.

"What are you going to do?"

"For now, we need to get Marnie fixed."

Monty returns with Benji, who rushes right over after being filled in on what was going on. He works fast, getting an IV drip started almost immediately. He also gets a bag of blood going. While he's doing that, I irrigate the wounds with the warm water.

Myself, Lita and Benji work simultaneously on the wounds that Kieran inflicted. While Lita and I aren't very good with a needle and thread, Benji carefully guides us through the process. And as the evening ticks by, the three of us manage to stitch up every wound. We wrap all of the freshly stitched wounds before dressing her in an oversized shirt. We then gently move her onto a stretcher for easier transport.

"How did this happen?" Benji asks as we pack away all of the medical supplies and throw away the bloody towels and tissues.

"The King. The scheming bastard is losing his head and Marnie paid part of the price for it."

"Shit."

"Yeah."

"What are you going to do?" Lita asks, drawing my attention away from Benji.

"I need you to get Carlos out of the palace. I'm going to need him. Then I want you, Lita, to grab

Mauro and start rounding up my team leaders and their staff. I want everyone in the Hutch tomorrow morning at half six."

"I'll get on it now. Do you want me to tell your people in the palace, or just Carlos?"

"Just Carlos. Everyone else will see the results soon enough." She smiles at me.

"Good luck."

"And to you."

CHAPTER FIVE

I haven't slept at all.

Lita left in the early hours of the morning while I stayed with Marnie. Benji stayed too, performing half hourly checks on her to make sure her condition was improving. And it has been, steadily. So right now, Benji and I are moving Marnie back to Lita's cottage via the stretcher we placed her on earlier. The streets are still relatively quiet at half five in the morning. There's no Police Patrols wandering the streets and there's no onlookers since the curfews are still in effect.

"Do you want me to stay with her?" Benji asks as we carefully manoeuvre ourselves through the cottage.

"If you could. I shouldn't be gone too long."

He nods. "I'll change her dressings and keep pumping her with fluids. I'll start a course of antibiotics as well. Last thing she needs is an infection," he says as we lift the stretcher onto the bed.

"I'll give you a quick tour before I head out."

I give Benji a tour before grabbing my bag and heading out.

The Hutch is in the more run down area of the island. It's an old village hall that we've been working on restoring so that it can be used recreationally. Similar to a lot of the buildings in this area, they're all run down and abandoned. But that's where my group comes in, restoring and caring for the island. Restoring it to what it used to be like before King Kieran started getting paranoid. That's the reason this is the most run down area of the island, he evacuated everyone, forced them to find new homes. For close to six years, this place was left to rot. Until now.

Once there, I remove the boards from the front, our best attempt at a deterrent for vandals and nosy Patrols. I slip inside, having to take a minute because a shooting pain in my stomach renders me immobile.

Once I manage to compose myself, I replace the boards at the front of the Hutch.

I set out three rows of tightly packed chairs so that anyone who needs a chair, has one. The rest can bunch up behind. The meeting won't be very long, so there's no need for everyone to sit down.

I yawn, feeling the tiredness finally set in. I can't remember the last time I had a proper night's sleep, so I take a seat on one of the chairs. I let my head tip back as I close my eyes and fall into a light sleep.

※

"Fallon?"

"Huh, what?" I say as I jump from my chair.

"Everyone's here," says Lita, gesturing to the room where people have started to file in.

"Right. Yes, thank you." I stand up and brush the invisible dirt from my trousers before straightening my blouse and jacket. I go over to the box I placed down earlier. I step onto it and wait until everyone stops talking.

"I called you all here today to ask for your help.

A little over a month ago, King Kieran left me for dead in the basement of the palace. If Marnie, Lita and Carlos hadn't found me when they did, I would've died. This all happened after Kat told her parents about our relationship."

"Is that why both of you haven't been around?" someone in the front row asks.

I nod. "While I was recovering, it seems that the royal family have all but locked Kat, and themselves, in the palace. It's concerning to say the least, limited contact has been made with my people on the inside, and those who have made contact don't have any information that can help me. As for Kat, no one has been able to get close enough to her to know how she's coping with all of this. But right now, I know that if she is in the palace then she is protected to a certain extent.

"But late last night Marnie was attacked. Old Monty found her, and brought to the Rat and Mouse where myself, Lita, Carli, Monty and Benji worked to stitch her up."

"Is she okay?" Ella, one of my team leaders, asks.

I nod. "She's being monitored by Benji who is

positive she'll make a full recovery."

"Who attacked her?"

"The King. The same man who is meant to be looking after this Island is losing his mind. I briefly encountered King Kieran before my attack, and I noticed his symptoms getting worse. In a previous meeting I told you all to watch out for Police Patrols with strange orders, I want you to keep doing that. The King is losing himself, he's twitchy, unpredictable, and paranoid. He's sick, and no one is doing anything about it. Now is not the time to be caught out by strange regulations."

"How will we avoid them?"

"All eight of my team leaders will be paired with one of my contactable people inside the palace. They'll directly feed you information which you can use to plan your days accordingly, and to ensure that you have the correct papers on site. The next two weeks are going to be rough, so we need to be two steps ahead at all times," I explain, and everyone nods in agreement.

"What about Kat?"

"Kat is my world and I'm not going to let her

marry someone she doesn't want to. So we're going to stop the wedding."

The crowd murmurs, in what seems to be both concern and excitement. I know some will be worried about the idea of stopping a royal wedding. Interfering in Royal matters is an immediate arrest warrant on your name, but if we work together in a coordinated fashion, everything will be over before the King can even utter the words *arrest them all*.

"But how do we know that stopping the wedding will make everything better?"

"You need to trust in me. You need to trust in kat. You've all met her; you've seen the way she took interest in every single project. How she stood in front of you and said that when she was Queen, she would invest in us, in the Island. Katarina isn't her father's copy, she's her own person, with her own beliefs and her own plans for the island. She is a person of the people, and she would do anything for all of you."

They are all silent for a moment.

"I support you," says one of my team leaders as she steps forward.

"I do as well." Another team leader raises their

hand.

"So do I."

One by one, everyone steps up with murmurs of support. They chant and cheer for Kat, for the future of the island. I've never felt prouder of this group than I do right now.

CHAPTER SIX

We work hard on the plan for stopping the royal wedding. It takes us a week and six days. My team leaders have been coaching and guiding their teams through their designated distractions, and I couldn't be happier with the results I've seen.

Tomorrow is the wedding and so far, six of the eight distractions are ready to mobilise. My job for today is to check on the final two distractions which are, by far, the most important. The idea is to cause as much chaos as possible so that the Royal Guards and Police Patrols are forced to move away from the front of the church.

I turn onto Stripene Avenue and find Group Five working on their distraction. Group Five is filled with mothers and fathers who cannot afford childcare or cannot find a space at one of the day-cares in the upper end of the Island. The work I have them do allows them to have their children with them. It provides the parents with a safe place, and safe adult, to look after their children while they work. While other groups rebuild buildings across the island, Group Five renovate the insides with fresh paint, furniture and decor.

"How's it going?" I ask Stephanie, the team leader.

"It's going extremely well. The karts are coming along nicely, and the kids can't wait to drive them."

The plan for their distraction is the kids, aged between eight and fifteen, being given roughly built karts that they will be racing round the Prepor Hills. They'll be roughly made which should catch the attention of the patrols since they won't meet the legal requirements for drivable karts. But we've ensured that they're safe enough for the kids so that they won't get hurt.

"Glad to hear it. All on schedule?"

"All on schedule and we'll be moving them between patrol passes."

I nod. "Good. Carlos will coordinate with you in the morning. Once you're all done and the Patrols come, I'll need you to join me in the church."

"I'll be there. Since we're the first group to set off our distractions, I'll help coordinate getting the other leaders to the church."

"Sounds perfect, thank you, Steph."

"Any time. If you need anything else, just let me know."

I give her an appreciative smile. "I need to go and check on Group Six, so I'll leave you to it. Keep up the good work."

I head back through the town and down Stick Road, following it all the way to the docks. The island isn't terribly big. It'll take you no longer than forty five minutes to walk shoreline to shoreline. It makes it easier for me to check on all of my active work sites in one day, and getting between the north and the south docks is no different. A decent chunk of the money my father left me has been going into making the docks a lot more functional. Being able to use the docks in their full capacity would mean an influx of imports. We'd be able to accept more tourists since we could have multiple boats a day compared to the one a week we welcome at the moment. We could also be utilising the trading routes far more than we do now.

"Fallon," shouts Chrissy, the daughter of the dockmaster, when she sees me. She bounds up the decking before flinging her arms around me.

"Hi Chrissy. How's everything going?" I ask, returning the hug. It only lasts a few seconds before we walk along the decking toward her father's post.

"It's going well. All the fireworks are in place and set to go off on the timers."

"What about the ones further inland?"

"They're set and ready to go off at ten on the dot."

"Brilliant. You guys have done some really good work here. And the docks are looking amazing, you should be proud of yourselves."

"Thanks, Fal. That means a lot."

I smile at her. "I need to go. I've got two more stops to make before tomorrow." I look out over the water and see the sun beginning to set, which means it's nearly time for the most crucial part of the plan.

"But keep up the good work. I'll see you tomorrow."

"Good luck," she says as she hugs me again.

"Thank you," I say as I walk off, heading in the direction of the cottage.

∗

When I arrive at the cottage, Lita is waiting for me outside.

"Are you ready?" I nod.

"How long?"

"Ten minutes, max."

I nod.

We walk along the edge of the hill that the palace is on. We bypass Royal Guard Patrols before ducking under the vibrant bushes the gardeners spent hours planting last summer. We then sneak inside of the old tunnel, one that was forgotten about years ago. It was supposed to be blocked off after the palace staff stopped using it, but no one ever got round to it.

We take the first left and follow the hallway till we reach the steps that take us into the old library. A few years ago, a fire ravaged part of the castle after a guard fell asleep. He knocked a candle onto one of the carpet runners and it instantly caught fire. It destroyed a decent chunk of the library, corridor and part of the stairs. No one visits it anymore due to health and safety concerns, but that didn't stop me from using it almost every night when I came to visit Kat.

"Do you have everything set?"

"Yes."

"Nervous?"

"What do you think?" I question just as the door swings open to reveal Carlos and Kat.

It takes Kat a second, but as she finishes gazing around the library, our eyes lock and she gasps. "Fal?"

She closes the gap between us, and I instantly reach out, pulling her close to me. Her arms wrap tightly around my neck as mine wrap around her waist.

"Hey."

"Are you really here?"

"Yes."

"Thank god," she mutters as her hands come up to cup my face before she pulls me down so that she can kiss me. She sighs as soon as our lips touch and I move one of my hands up and into her hair, pulling her as close as possible. I don't know how long we kiss for, but I curl my fingers into the hair at the nape of her neck and pull her back gently. I rest my forehead against hers. Seeing her again has my chest tightening as now I can see what the weeks apart have done to her. Her hair hasn't retained its tight ringlets. It's become frizzy and there are some tangles. Her skin has dulled a little, and it's clear she's not been sleeping. But she's still her, the most beautiful girl I've ever seen. The girl who I fell in love with.

"He– he said you died. That he made sure you wouldn't interfere with the family ever again," she whispers, tears slipping down her face.

"Hey, there's no need to cry. I'm here, I'm fine."

"Can I see it?"

"What?"

"The wound."

I go to object, but she stops me.

"Please, I need to see it. I need–" I cut her off with a kiss before taking a step back. I carefully lift up the hem of my shirt. The wound has mostly healed, leaving a small amount of scabbing and a decent scar. She gasps, her hands coming up to cover her mouth. After a few seconds, I tuck in my shirt back in.

"He hurt you," she whimpers, and I instantly pull her into me, holding her tightly with my hand cupping the back of her head.

"I know, but he won't get the chance again. I promise you."

"What about Marnie? She came to see me and then she– she just disappeared."

"Your dad, he attacked her. But Old Monty found her, and we got her to Benji just in time. She's going to be fine."

She nods. I kiss the crown of her head. We're silent for a while, just soaking in the time together. I've missed her more than I could ever put into words. This girl is it for me, and I'm never letting her go again.

"I don't want to marry Miles."

"I know. That's why I'm here. My team and I have a plan."

"Really? What is it?"

I lean down to her ear and whisper what I need

from her. She doesn't say anything until I pull away from her ear and look her in the eyes.

"Yes."

"Good. I'll see you soon." I kiss her one more time before heading toward the door.

"Fal?" she calls as I open the door.

"Yes?"

"I love you."

I smile at her. "I love you more."

CHAPTER SEVEN

Spending time with Kat last night made me even more determined to fix everything. To get her on the throne, and her father off of it.

I sit on top of one of Prepor Hills, Stick Road directly underneath me. I watch the water ripple, the waves crashing against the shoreline and the sun gently rising above the horizon. The calm before the storm.

If all of this works, then I'm going to finish what my father started. The money that my father left me was syphoned from investments that were based on the Mainland and the surrounding Territories. It was done by a man named Paul Eatons, a man who was close to my father. Both of them knew that the Island needed that money more than the Territories did. For forty years, Paul carefully skimmed money from those projects and placed it in an account that he would access later. Unfortunately, Paul passed before he could use the money. That's when my father took control of the account and left a note that declared I was only to gain access to the money if anything were to happen to him. And when it did happen, I took control. No matter how hard the grief of losing him hit me, I had to carry on. The Island needed that money, and it needed the help my father's group was trying to provide.

It pains me to think about it, but I know that the King had something to do with the accident that killed him. There was nothing obvious out of place at the scene, but it was too clean. Too perfect. My father was healthy as anything, not a single medical emergency his entire life. Once all of this is over, I'm going to open an investigation into his death. I want to bring him justice and punish those who thought they could get away with killing him.

"Are you ready?" Carlos asks, drawing my attention away from my memories.

I nod.

"Everyone else ready?"

"They're awaiting the signal." I get up from where I'm sitting, taking a final look at the rising sun.

"Let's go."

※

Ten - oh - clock arrives fairly quickly once Carlos and I reach the centre of the Island. Carlos peels off toward his assigned area, while I join Lita on the top balcony of the cathedral. We stand there, overlooking the wedding parade.

As the royal carriages pass by, I wait until they turn the final corner toward the church before sending the signal to Group Six. There's a few moments of delay before bright fireworks light up the sky. The crowds watching the parade *ooh* and *ahh*, and they start to look for the source of the fireworks. The second lot of fireworks go off, lighting up the roofs directly overhead and it's just enough to spook the Guards and Police.

I watch as Carlos sends the next signal to Group Five. He uses the mirror, that Mauro set up yesterday afternoon, and three flashes of light bounce off the top window of Prepor Hills Castle. To confirm they got the signal, Stephanie sends back three flashes of her own. I look toward Prepor just as the karts start racing toward the parade. The Guards struggle to stop all the karts. Their shouts for help fill the streets, which makes the Police from the front and side entrances of the church to rush over. Lita and I take this chance to slip back into the cathedral before heading across the road and into the church.

We carefully mix in with the guests who still have yet to take a seat. We make small talk with certain guests and say polite hellos to members of the church.

"How many do you count?" I ask Carlos, referencing my team leaders who should already be inside by now. Prior to today, each of my leaders was sent a hat or blazer so that they could be easily identified.

"Four on our side," he says as I sit next to him.

"Good, four on the opposite side."

"All your contacts here?" he asks.

"Yep. Looks like we're good to go."

The *contacts* in my network are those who managed to get themselves into the Royal's Personal Guard. They worked hard to be considered for the Personal Guard, since it was the only Guard role that would keep them in a close proximity to Kat at all times. They would report back to me with her movements and routine so that I knew when she was free. They also helped me get into the palace late at night to surprise her, and their presence made me feel more comfortable during the times she was with her father and Miles.

A nudge to my shoulder has me turning to face Lita.

"What?" I whisper to her.

"She's here." Just as she finishes speaking, the organ starts playing and everyone in the church stands up.

The flower girls walk by first, all of them dressed in the same baby purple dresses. Their hair has tied back with elastic bands and decorated with baby's breath crowns. They all have woven baskets in their hands and are scattering pretty rose petals along the white tiles. The bridesmaids follow closely behind.

Six of them filter down the aisle before taking up their places on what will be Kat's side of the alter. They all look elegant, and the epitome of high society; but the lustful gaze's they are throwing at Miles suggests that they wouldn't waste any time in trying taking him from Kat. Why they would want him though, I'll never understand, but they'll be welcome to him very shortly.

Then Kat starts to walk down the aisle. Her father is gripping onto their linked arms, practically dragging her along behind him. Her dress is bright white, plain, and the kind a conservative and rule obeying royal would wear. It looks nothing like the dress she described to me when we spoke about getting married. She told me she wanted to wear a dress with a sweetheart neckline and off the shoulder sleeves that would've been made of the daintiest material. It would have lace detailing and would be a baby blue coloured material. She'd gotten out of bed and grabbed her sketch book, flipped through it and showed me the drawing of it. It would suit her down to the ground and would look ten times better than the one she's wearing right now.

Kieran guides her up the steps and stops in front of the altar. He unlinks their arms and places Kat's hands in Miles's. Everyone retakes their seats, and we wait for the Officiant to take up his place.

CHAPTER EIGHT

The Officiant steps forward.

"Family, friends, associates. We've gathered here today, together in the view of the Star, to witness and celebrate the union of Princess Katarina Greenfled of Molleni Island and Associated Territories, and Prince Miles Dylani of Ordol," he says, addressing the church and the radio broadcast channel.

Everyone sits and listens to him talk. Everyone takes in every word that comes out of his mouth, except me. My attention is solely focused on Kat and the way she keeps squirming and shuffling from foot to foot. I can feel her discomfort from here and it makes me wish I could step in right now, but I can't. I have to wait for the right moment.

"And now, for the vows. The bride and groom

have chosen to give traditional vows. Miles, would you like to start."

Miles nods. "I, Miles Dylani, take you, Katarina Greenfled, to be my wife. I promise to be faithful to you, in the good times and in the bad, during sickness and in health. To love you and to honour you the rest of my life."

"Katarina, your turn."

She nods. "I, Katarina Greenfled, take you." She pauses, taking a deep breath. "Miles Dylani, to be my husband. I promise to be faithful to you, in the good times and in the bad, during sickness and in health. To love you and to honour you for the rest of my life."

The Officiant nods. "Now, I must ask if anyone has any reason to object to the union of these two people."

The crowd waits silently, their eyes subtly darting around the room, waiting to catch sight of someone who is willing to interfere in a royal wedding. No one from my group moves until my gaze lands on the Officiant. As he goes to open his mouth, to utter the words that will take Kat away from me forever, I jump up from my seat.

"I object." The crowd behind me gasps.

This time, I lock eyes with the King. I watch the colour drain from his face as he rises from his throne. I watch his eye twitch and his hands reach for imaginary weapons.

"Guards, seize her," King Kieran screeches.

"No, not yet." The Officiant hold up his hand, halting any sudden movements from both the Guards and King Kieran. "Why do you object to the union of these two people, miss…"

"Fallon Edington. I object because Katarina Greenfled is my wife," I say as I make my way over to Kat. I remove her hand from Miles's and clasp it tightly. I take out the ring I've been keeping in my pocket and slip it onto her left hand.

"*Your* wife?" Kieran spits.

"*My* wife."

CHAPTER NINE

"That's not true. There's no possible way you two can be married," he seethes as he approaches us. "I killed you. I. Killed. You."

I ignore him and the sudden murmurs from the wedding guests. "In the early hours of this morning, a local church Officiant married us. We were surrounded by our friends and loved ones." I take the rolled up marriage licence and certificate from Carlos. I show them to Kieran and the Officiant.

"I told you, dad. I tried to tell you that I love Fallon, but you didn't listen," Kat says as she tries to reason with her father. He's taking deep breaths while his body twitches. His hands clench and unclench and his whole body tenses. He's trying to control himself. It's obvious he's finally lost control as he launches himself at us. Luckily, my team leaders step in and pull at Kieran's arms before Royal Guards take over.

"You're not well, dad. Even now, you've shown that you are not in control of yourself. My father, my healthy father, wouldn't try and attack me for giving my views. For following my heart."

"I am in control. Katarina you are being brainwashed by this Edington girl. She's a liar, just like her father."

"I am not brainwashing anyone. Sir, you are unwell. You need professional help, and we have people who can help you. Contacts on the Associated Territories are willing to help you get better," I tell him. He tries to lunge at us again, but the Guards holding him are much stronger.

"Dad, please. Just listen to us. You are unwell. Everyone in the palace has seen it. Even mother has noticed but she told me she would never tell anyone about it. You need *help*. I didn't want it to come to this, but it's time someone called you out for your behaviour. It's time someone took charge and got you the help that you need."

"Camille, control our daughter," he yells.

Camille rushes over and tries to intervene. The three of them start arguing. Even Miles tries to butt in, but Kat doesn't let him. She stands her ground.

"We called an emergency Elder meeting this morning. We've informed them of what's been going on and they will be removing you from power with immediate effect. As of this moment I am the Queen of Molleni, with an official coronation taking place a week tomorrow."

"NO. I am your King–"

Guards filter past us, led by Benji. The guards escort Kieran out to the carriage waiting behind the church. We secured it there earlier this morning after consulting with Benji. He agreed to escort Kieran to a hospital on the Mainland where I've arranged treatment with the best doctor money could fund. Camille wastes no time in chasing after her husband.

The church is silent until the doors at the back of the building slam shut. Then chaos ensues. The crowd begins murmuring again, and I'd almost forgotten that we have an audience. I gaze over the crowd, my eyes land on Kat. She's stepped away from me and is having a very intense conversation with Miles.

I step closer, my hand gently grazing her lower back. "Everything alright?"

"Yes. I'm just letting Miles know that the engagement is over."

"I will be notifying the Elders of the Territories. This will not go unpunished," he seethes.

"The Elders have already been informed and they are more than happy with our union. There will be no action taken by the Elders," Kat explains.

"Go home, Miles," I order, cutting him off from arguing any further. He scoffs and storms in the direction of the back door.

"That felt too easy," Kat says as she all but falls into my arms.

"If he comes back, we'll deal with it."

She nods and then looks over the crowd.

"Do they look angry? I feel like they're angry," she whispers. I shake my head and kiss her temple.

"Guess it's time for you to take control. To speak to your people," I mutter in her ear.

"What do I say?"

"Reassure them. Tell them what you told my team the night we went to the Winter Festival."

She nods and steps forward. Everyone is instantly quiet.

"I know all of you must be confused, and maybe even worried, but I want to trust me. I want you to have faith in me. My father isn't well, he hasn't been for quite some time. He was good at hiding it, but he has been losing control of himself. And while, as a family, we tried to help him, nothing worked. He refused help from us and those around him who were willing to give it to him. It all came to a head when my father made plans for my marriage with Prince Miles, and after telling him I wanted to marry Fallon, he stabbed her."

Everyone gasps and murmurs break out across the church.

"He left her to die, but her people saved her. The people who Fallon works with are helping to renovate the Island. They are working to rebuild what my father neglected to care about. And for my first act as Queen, I will be investing in the wellness of the Island, into the infrastructure and the economy. All of this will come before I consider where the investments into the Territories and Mainland go. I plan on rectifying what my father refused to in his declining state, and that means starting at the heart of our home."

Everyone claps and cheers for Kat. They all rise from their seats and chant for her.

"You did great," I say as I kiss her forehead. "I'm so proud of you."

"You really think so?"

"Yes. Look."

The audience in front of us has moved so that they're on one knee, with a hand raise over their heart.

"Oh god," she mutters as she looks at her supporters. "Is all of that for me?"

"Yes, Your Highness. All of it and so much more."

"I feel dizzy, and slightly sick," she says while laughing. I bite my lip as a manner of different emotions bubbles up inside of me. Pride, love and admiration for Kat. I'm so proud of how far she has come. She never would have stood against her father before our relationship began, she wouldn't have had the guts to do this. But she's grown so much in the last year, and I couldn't be prouder of her.

I turn to the crowd and gracefully lift one of Kat's arms.

"To your Queen of Molleni."

"To Her Royal Highness, Queen Katarina of Molleni."

CHAPTER TEN

Over the last six days, the whole Island has been preparing for Kat's coronation.

Everything has been chaotic as we've worked to settle the sceptics and the political powers of our surrounding Territories. It turns out, Kieran had stopped most of his in person meetings with political powers across the Territories. He would only communicate through letters and would send his Attendings in his place if someone demanded an in person meeting. He knew he wasn't well but was determined to carry on as though nothing was wrong. To hide what was going on behind the scenes which ultimately did more harm than good.

The last three days have had us working with the other Territories to establish new and stronger trade lines. We've shown them the work that Chrissy and the team have done, and how the money I put back into developing the docks will allow us to cater to more visitors and merchant ships. We've also secured four new five year trading contracts, contracts which will benefit everyone in the long and short term. We've also secured extra funding to help us renovate the whole island. The Territory leaders seem like good people, especially with how willing they are to help us get the Island back to the shape it was before all of this started. Years of deterioration have left permanent scars across the Island, but we're finally heading in the right direction. We're finally healing.

"Why are you thinking so hard?" Kat asks, bringing me out of my head.

"I'm just thinking about everything," I admit.

We're lying in bed, tucked nicely under the duvet. She's cuddled up to my right side and I've got my left hand behind my head. We've not been awake long, but we know that sometime in the next ten minutes, Lita will burst into the room and force us out of bed.

"Don't stress yourself too much," she says before

snuggling back down under the duvet.

I pull her closer and press my lips to her hairline. We've barely left each other since the failed wedding. We've gone to every meeting together, to every consultation and infrastructure meeting. I'd have been much more content with letting her go to them alone, but she wouldn't let me out of her sight for more than a bathroom break. I guess being forcefully separated and being made to believe that I was dead has made her want to know that I'm fine all the time. That I'm never going to leave her again, and that is something I don't plan on doing, *ever*.

"I love you," I say, kissing her. "I love you more than you'll ever know. And nothing is ever going to keep us apart, you understand?"

"I do, I understand. I just sometimes feel like you're going to disappear. That I'll blink and Miles will be there, waiting."

I shake my head and manoeuvre us so that I'm hovering over her. "Miles is gone. He's in the past and licking his wounds. You don't need to worry about anything. It's just you and me. The Queen and Queen Consort."

She giggles. "What if I made you Queen?"

"What?"

She rolls us back over so that she's straddling my hips. "What if I got rid of the Consort part. We're equals in our relationship, so I don't want the slightest difference between us when we're working. Even if it is just a title."

I look up at her, shocked. "Are you sure? I'm not much of a Queen. And this is something you've trained your whole life for."

"I want you to be Queen alongside me. Please?"

"I don't know–"

"Please? Pretty, pretty, pretty please, Fal?" she begs, giving me her best puppy dog eyes. I shake my head playfully, ready to say yes, but she carries on begging.

"Please, Fallon. I'll make it worth your while." She runs her fingers down my sternum and across to my shoulders.

I grab her hands in mine, lacing our fingers together before lifting myself with all my might so that I tip us back over so that I'm on top.

"I was going to say yes, flat out, but now you've

given me the offer of making it worth my while." I lean down and kiss her again, harder this time. The tips of my fingers find the edge of her night shirt before they graze the skin of her hips. She sighs just as the door to our bedroom slams against the wall, no doubt leaving a dent.

"Time to get– Oh, god. Could you two not," Lita exclaims as I look up to find her covering her eyes.

"This is our room. We can do whatever we want here," I say as I roll off of Kat and get out of the bed.

"Yeah, but every time I come in here you two are making out," she rants, heading into our shared wardrobe. I follow her.

"Well, we are newlyweds, and this is our room, with our bed. A place where we can do whatever we want–"

"Yada, yada, yada. With the best will in the world, I don't want to know the ins and outs of what goes on in your bedroom."

I laugh and leave the wardrobe, heading back over to the bed. I pull Kat out of bed, and she instantly wraps her arms around me.

"What's up?"

"Just nervous."

"I'm here with you, forever. You've got nothing to be nervous about," I tell her as I place a kiss on the crown of her head.

Lita pulls out our outfits. She orders us to get showered and change into a clean set of underwear before thrusting dressing gowns into our arms. We quickly shower. Kat goes in first and then I hop in after her. When we emerge from the bathroom, Carlos and Marnie have joined Lita.

Marnie escorts Kat into our wardrobe, while Carlos and Lita stay with me. For the next half an hour Lita works on my hair, while Carlos works on my jewellery selection and make up. Lita curls my hair into coils before letting it all fall down my back. Carlos carefully clips two necklaces around my neck and slips many rings onto my fingers. Eventually, he hands me my nicely pressed blouse and trousers. I slip the trousers on underneath the dressing gown before undoing the belt and swapping the silky material for the chiffon blouse.

Lita then hands me the special ceremonial jacket I'm supposed to wear. It's heavy, and definitely not something I would wear if I was given the choice. Although, I do love the colour of it, deep, royal blue material makes up the main coat with accents of gold and red. It's decorated with gold jewellery and the signet of Molleni.

"Shoes," Carlos says as he hands me my favourite boots. Worn leather, gently polished with three buckles at the top and zip.

"Thanks. How do I look?"

"Like a badass Queen Consort should."

I smile. "Actually, I'm not the Queen Consort, Kat wants to make me Queen by title. Said she didn't want anything to a divide us."

"That's adorable," Lita says as she steps away from the wardrobe.

Kat steps out. She's dressed in a beautiful blue gown, draped in her ceremonial sash and cape. Her hair has been pinned back neatly, with her wispy baby hairs styled and framing her face.

"Kat, you look stunning," I say, stepping forward and taking her face in my hands. "How are you feeling?"

"Thank you. I'm nervous, but I know I can do it

because you'll be there with me."

"Damn right." I lean in to kiss her but Marnie interrupts.

"You will not kiss Katarina. Her makeup is done, and I will not have you ruin it."

"You're no fun," I pout.

She waves me off before heading out of the room, muttering something about making sure the carriage is here. Lita and Carlos follow behind her, giving us some time alone.

"I'm proud of you for stepping up and taking on your fathers role. I know your mother has been fighting you about how everything went down, but I want you to know that I'm so proud of you."

She sniffles. "Thank you, but if you make me cry my makeup will run and then Marnie will kill you."

I laugh. "If your father couldn't kill me, Marnie hasn't a chance in hell."

Kat laughs and shakes her head. Then she rises up on her tiptoes and gently presses her lips to mine.

"I love you, Kat, and I can't wait for the rest of our lives."

A. Carys

Want to witness Fallon and Kat's wedding?

Turn the page to find out how and where it happened…

THE ENGAGEMENT

Watching Fallon leave makes my heart hurt, but knowing what we're about to do makes me feel so much better. It makes me feel hopeful for my future.

She's given me one hour to get ready and meet her at the Rat and Mouse. Lita stays with me until Fallon is out of sight. Then she grabs my hand and pulls me back through the tunnels, all the way to the old door in the back of my wardrobe. I close it behind us and tuck the curtain back over it to keep it hidden from prying eyes.

"What do you want to wear?" Lita asks as she looks at the dresses that line the walls.

"I don't mind. What about this one?" I say as I pull out a beautiful pale blue chiffon dress. It's flowy and light. I've only worn it once, and that was for one of the dates Fallon took me on at the beginning of our relationship.

"It looks perfect. Let me get the pins for your hair." She disappears out of the wardrobe, leaving me in privacy.

First I slip on a pair of dusty blue ballet slippers. I take off my nightgown and quickly put on a bra and an underskirt. I slip the dress on over my head before sorting it out so that the waist sits nicely. I step out of the wardrobe and look for Lita.

"Wow, you look stunning," she says as she scans my outfit.

"Thank you. Could you tie the corset at the back please?"

She nods and disappears behind me. I hold the top of the dress against my body as I feel her thread the ribbons at the back. She pulls it tight and then ties it in a bow.

"Come sit," she says as she pulls me gently toward the vanity.

I take a seat and Lita starts fixing my hair. I close my eyes and relax as she works on my hair.

I'm getting married. Tonight. To Fallon

Edington.

I almost can't believe it. I figured that if we ever got married, it was going to be after I was made Queen and could divorce Miles without the Elders and my father's opinion holding such a great weight. But we're doing it now, and I couldn't be happier, and the Elders couldn't be happier for us either. Their approval was given, and an in person meeting will happen after the ceremony.

I'm going to marry the love of my life.

"All done. You ready?" Lita asks as I open my eyes.

"So ready." I sneak a glance in the mirror before following her. My hair is neatly pinned at the back of my head with baby's breath flowers weaved into the updo. She's framed my face with wispy fly aways while the rest of curls have been revived.

"Lita, thank you," I say as I pull her in for a hug. I hold her tightly as a way of saying thank you.

"You're welcome, princess. Now come on, can't keep your future wife waiting."

✽

We reach the Rat and Mouse at midnight.

Carlos is waiting for us outside the establishment, a bouquet of flowers in his hands.

"These are for you. Fallon said lavender, roses and bluebells were your favourite." He hands me the bouquet and I nearly melt at the mention of Fallon remembering my favourite flowers.

"They're perfect."

"Well, the petal aisle awaits you," he says before slipping inside.

"'Bout time you two tied the knot," says Old Monty as he joins me outside.

"It's been a long time coming."

"Could I do the honours of walking you down the aisle, Miss Katarina?"

"I would love that, Monty, thank you," I say as we link arms. Lita opens the door for us, and we step inside.

Just as Carlos had mentioned, a rose petal aisle awaits me. The vibrant red petals have been scattered across the floor. The walls have been draped in long stemmed flowers and an archway has been erected in front of the dart wall.

"Wow," I murmur as I take everything in, and my eyes finally land on Fallon.

Her hair is tied back in its usual plaits and she's wearing her favourite trousers paired with a baby blue blouse. She's left the top few buttons of her shirt undone, and her jewellery sparkles as it catches the light. The lamplight also catches on her skin, and she looks like a Goddess. *My Goddess*.

"Take care of her. She might look and act tough, but she needs someone to look out for her," Monty whispers to me before placing my hands in Fallon's.

"I promise I'll take care of her."

He nods and heads over to one of the chairs that has been put out. I look at the audience and it's a small crowd. Lita, Marnie, Carlos, Monty, Carli and Mauro. My gaze lingers on Marnie for a second, taking in the fact that my father tried to kill her as well. That is something I will never forgive him for, nor will I forgive him for what he did to Fallon. Despite that though, they're both here. Fallon standing in front of me, and Marnie sitting a few feet away looking healthy.

"You look stunning," Fallon whispers to me.

"Thank you. So do you."

She smiles and nods as the Officiant starts her speech.

"Family, friends. We've gathered here today, together in the view of the Star, to witness and celebrate the union of Katarina Greenfled and Fallon Edington," she says and the urge to bounce on my toes with happiness surges through me.

"The couple have their own vows that they would like to read instead. Fallon?"

"Kat, the evening we met, I'd never wanted to be in such close quarters to a person. I've spent the last five years of my life bossing people around and working to ensure that their quality of life is improved. I'd spent that time settling into a routine, a lonely routine with only one focus. Everyone else. But when we met, a spark ignited inside of me, one that I knew was never going to be extinguished because I wasn't going to let you go. Ever.

"Every date we went on had me falling deeper and deeper in love with you and I knew that you were the one for me. The only girl I want to spend my life with. I love you, Kat, and I vow to spend the rest of my days proving that to you. I will take care of you. I will take interest in everything you care about. I vow to support you in everything you do, and I vow to be the partner you need."

"Thank you, Fallon. Katarina, your turn."

I take a deep breath and try to swallow the lump that's formed in my throat from trying not to cry at Fallon's vows.

"Well, I'm going to wing this since I found out about this wedding an hour ago. Fallon you are my rock. The girl who I shoved into the gravel as she tried to rob me. A girl who, at the time, I didn't know would change my life for the better. The day we met; you awoke a part of me that I never would've discovered if I'd stayed in the palace that night. Instead, I went against the orders of my parents and went to see the festival in person. And then I met you and you opened my eyes to a whole new world. You showed me what love was meant to be like, and you taught me how to be true to myself.

"I love you. I love your work ethic and your need to better the island. I vow to work alongside you to ensure that we do the best we can for the people. I love that you've helped me become the best version of myself, a version I wouldn't have become without you. So I vow to love you until my last breath and to support you no matter what. I love you, Fallon, and marrying you is only a technicality in our relationship since I believe you're my soulmate. You're it for me."

"Thank you, Katarina. Now, for the rings."

Monty gets up from his chair and brings over a small box. He opens it and hands me one ring, while giving the other to Fallon. Fallon goes first, slipping her ring onto my left hand before I slip mine onto hers. Mine has a little diamond in the middle of a dainty flower while Fallon's is a band with an engraving on the inside.

"By the power vested in me, I now pronounce you wife and wife. Congratulations, and you may kiss the bride."

The Officiant steps back and Fallon takes a step forward. Her hands come up to my face and she pulls me into her, catching my lips in a deep kiss. My hands instantly wrap around her neck, pulling her down to me. Fireworks explode inside of me, and my heart feels so full of love and happiness. I can faintly hear our small crowd of friends clapping and celebrating. All of a sudden, Fallon's hands come to waist, and she dips me, never once letting our lips part.

"Love you," she murmurs.

"I love you more."

She pulls away and looks me in the eyes.

"Tomorrow, we'll take back the island, and you'll become Queen."

I nod. "My parents will fight me about it."

"You won't need to worry because I'll be there the whole time. We're in this together."

I nod and press a chaste kiss to her lips.

"Together."

ABOUT THE AUTHOR

A. Carys is a self-published author from Portsmouth, United Kingdom. Other than spending 90% of her day writing, she also loves to crochet, read, and take photos of her family's cats.

Printed in Great Britain
by Amazon